Passport
to Paris

Penn Mullin

High Noon Books
Novato, California

Cover Design and Interior Illustrations: Damon Rarey

International Standard Book Number: 0-87879-978-8

9 8 7 6 5 4 3 2
2 1 0 9 8 7 6 5 4

You'll enjoy all the High Noon Books. Write for
a free full list of titles.

Contents

All aboard! Justin, Juan, Amy, Miss Lake and Lisa.

It was a wonderful surprise for the four seventh graders in Miss Lake's class when they learned they had won a trip around the United States for their essays on "What Do You Like Best About Being an American?"

Then a mysterious "Mrs. X" read about them in the newspaper. She was so proud of them that she surprised them with an all-expenses-paid trip through Europe with their teacher!

Mrs. X has arranged a surprise for the group in each place they visit. But there is a catch. The surprise can be found only if the kids follow Mrs. X's clues. And the clues lead them to exciting famous places. Even finding their guide at the start of each trip is a mystery to be solved.

CHAPTER 1

A Clue at Breakfast!

"Please pass the *croissants* (cwassance)," said Juan. "Did I say that right?"

"Very good for your first day in Paris," laughed Miss Lake, his teacher. They were having breakfast at their hotel with Amy, Justin, and Lisa.

"Look! Here's our first clue! It's hidden in the basket under the *croissants*," said Justin. "I bet it's from our guide for Paris. It will tell us where to find him."

"Maybe it's a 'her' this time," Lisa said. "Hurry and open the envelope!"

"O.K. Hold on. Uh-oh. The first part is in French. I'm in trouble," Justin said. "But here goes!" He read aloud:

Bonjour, mes amis! (Good day, my friends)

Bienvenue à Paris! (Welcome to Paris)

Venez à L'Étoile (Come to *L'Étoile*)

Lundi à neuf heures (Monday at nine o'clock)

I'll be by the flame

And you'll learn my name!

"Good job, Justin," said Miss Lake. "Well, we have some good clues here. Does anyone know any of these French words?"

"*Lundi.* Is that Monday?" Amy asked.

"That's right! And that's today," Miss Lake said. "What time do we meet?"

"Does *neuf* mean nine?" Juan asked.

"Yes. So we meet today at nine. "And there is a place in Paris called *L'Étoile* (Lay-twoll). Get out your maps. Let's look for it."

The kids unfolded their maps of Paris.

"This is such a big city!" Justin said. "How will we ever find *L'Étoile*?"

"I see it!" Juan pointed to his map. "There is a big arch there."

"Right. That is called the *Arc de Triomphe*," said Miss Lake. "It sits in the center of twelve streets. And the streets look like the points of a star. *L'Étoile* means star. That must

3

be how *L'Étiole* got its name. Our guide will meet us there!"

"By the flame?" Lisa asked.

"You will see when you get there. We must start for the métro. It will soon be nine o'clock," Miss Lake said.

"Is the métro the subway?" Juan asked.

"Yes. We can ride all over Paris on it. And this hotel is near the station," their teacher said.

"I'm taking some *croissants* to snack on," Justin said. "These taste great!" He stuffed two of the golden brown rolls into his backpack.

"Your backpack is getting pretty full," Lisa laughed. "How many meals do you have in there now?"

"Just wait till you're hungry for a snack," Justin told her. "Then you'll wish you had all this." He patted his backpack.

"Whose turn is it to write a postcard to Mrs. X?" Miss Lake asked.

"Mine. Maybe I'll write it in French!" Justin laughed as he put on his backpack.

"Now that would be something else!" Juan said. "Poor Mrs. X!"

"Come on, kids! To the métro!" Miss Lake said.

The kids followed their teacher out into the busy Paris street. But Justin had to run to catch up. He had grabbed more *croissants* and couldn't get his backpack to close!

CHAPTER 2

To the Top of the World!

"Here comes the métro! I can hear it." Amy pointed into the dark tunnel ahead.

"It's so quiet. Why is that?" Justin asked. The train pulled up next to them.

"It has rubber wheels!" Miss Lake told them. "Hop on, everybody! Next stop is *L'Étoile*!"

The train rushed off into the darkness. They all watched the stations flash by.

Soon the train slowed down for the *L'Étoile*

stop. The kids and their teacher got off and went upstairs to the street.

"Wow! This place is huge!" Amy said.

They looked up at the high stone arch ahead of them. Cars were racing around and around it. Their engines roared.

"How can we get over to the arch?" Lisa shouted to Miss Lake.

"Here's a tunnel. Follow me," their teacher said. They went down under the streets and came up under the giant arch.

"How will we ever find our guide? There are a zillion people here!" Lisa said.

"By the flame. That's what the clue said." Juan pointed towards the center of the arch. A

Arc de Triomphe

small flame burned on the walkway under it. They started over there.

Suddenly they saw a tall smiling blond woman coming towards them. She held out her hand to Miss Lake.

"*Bienvenue à Paris!* (Welcome to Paris!) You found me! I am Nicole, your guide in this beautiful city." Nicole shook hands and found out all the names. "Madame X wants you to see everything in Paris. I will do my best!"

"You speak beautiful English," Miss Lake told their guide.

"Thank you! My mother was an American. That was a big help," Nicole said. "Well, I am happy I can show you my city. This is a good place to start. The *Arc de Triomphe* is the largest arch in the world. It is 154 feet high and 148 feet wide!"

"How old is it?" Justin asked.

"Have you heard of Napoléon Bonaparte? He was emperor of France in 1806. He had the arch built to honor his soldiers," Nicole said. "The carvings in the stone show many battles in French history."

"Why is the flame there?" Amy asked.

"To honor the Unknown Soldier of World War I," said Nicole. "He is buried under the Eternal Flame." Then she added, "Now I'm taking you to a fine place to see Paris – the Eiffel (Eyefull) Tower!" She pointed to the black tower rising high above the city.

"Hey, terrific! When do we go?" Justin asked. "It looks close by!"

"And awfully high!" said Lisa. "Maybe I can get a good view from just halfway up!"

"No way!" laughed Juan. "You're going to the top! There might be a clue up there!"

"You can bring it down to me!" said Lisa.

"This is a good time to talk about French history. Paris is full of it," Nicole said. "Let's start to the métro while we talk."

"I've heard about Marie Antoinette," Amy said. "Can you tell us about her?"

"She was the Queen of France, wife of King Louis the Sixteenth," Nicole said. "In

1789 they lived in luxury at a palace outside Paris called *Versailles* (ver-sigh). But the poor people of Paris were starving. And the king and queen didn't seem to care. Finally, the people got tired of this. They brought the king and queen into Paris and put them into prison at a palace called the *Louvre* (Louvra). And later they were beheaded."

"That's awful," Amy said.

"Isn't the Louvre a museum now?" Lisa asked.

"Yes, the most famous in the world. And you will see it today!" Nicole told the kids.

They all went into the métro tunnel.

"We get off at *Tour Eiffel*," Nicole said.

They stepped onto the subway.

"Were a lot of people beheaded?" Juan asked Nicole. "Can you see where the guillotine stood?"

"Yes, the king and queen were the first of nearly 1,400 people to die that way in the French Revolution," Nicole said. "And, yes, you can see right where the guillotine was."

"Creepy!" Lisa said.

"Does France still have a king?" Justin asked.

"No, it has a president. He rules with the help of a prime minister and a parliament," Nicole said. "No more kings."

"Here's our stop!" Miss Lake said.

They all got off and went up the stairs.

"Wow! There it is! That is really high!" Juan said as he looked up at the tower.

"Once the Eiffel Tower was the tallest building in the world," Nicole told them. "It is 984 feet high. But your Sears Tower in Chicago is taller!"

"How old is the tower?" Lisa asked.

"Afraid it will fall over?" Juan laughed.

"It is very strong. Don't worry," Nicole said. "It's been standing here since 1889."

"Can I stop halfway up?" Lisa asked.

"Yes, the elevator stops at three places. Wait and see how you feel," Nicole told her.

"Here, have a *croissant*. It will make your

Eiffel Tower

stomach feel better," Justin said.

"I can't believe it. You are parting with one of your *croissants,* Justin!" Lisa laughed.

"Well, you're a good clue-finder. We need you up on top," Justin said.

"Here's the elevator!" Mis Lake led the kids inside and Nicole followed.

"Whoa! Don't look down, Lisa," Amy said.

The elevator moved quickly up one of the four iron legs of the tower. Then it stopped.

"Lisa, stay on. This isn't high at all," Juan said. "Try the next platform."

Lisa kept looking straight up. The black iron pieces of the tower stretched high above. "I'm O.K. – so far," she said.

The elevator started up again. Now they were way above the trees. Paris was beginning to spread out below them.

"This city is so beautiful!" Miss Lake said. "Look how far you can see! Thank you, Mr. Eiffel, for building this tower!"

"Who was Mr. Eiffel?" Justin asked.

"Gustav Eiffel was the man who built this for the 1889 Paris World's Fair," Nicole said. "He never meant for it to last this long."

"*Now* you tell me," Lisa said.

"Don't worry, it is held together with two and a half million rivets!" Nicole said. "The tower was supposed to be taken down in 1890. That was when the fair ended. But by then it was very important for its radio antennae. That saved it. And today the French love their tower."

The elevator stopped again. "This is where I get off," Lisa said. "High enough."

"Oh, no, Lisa, stay on. You can see 50 miles on a day like today," Nicole told her.

"But I can feel it swaying already!" said Lisa. "Uh oh, we're already moving again!"

"Just keep thinking about the clue that's up there!" Justin told her.

The elevator pulled them steadily up to the top of the tower. Finally it stopped. They all stepped out onto a walled deck.

"Amazing!" Juan whistled. He looked out

over the city. "It's like we're in a plane!"

Lisa stayed right by the elevator door. "I'm not going near the edge," she said.

"What is that white church way up on the hill?" Amy asked Nicole.

"It is called *Sacré Coeur* (sacray cur), Sacred Heart. The hill is called *Monmartre* (mohmart). This is a beautiful part of Paris. You can see many artists working outside up there. We will visit it later on," Nicole said.

"Is that river the Seine (senne)?" Amy asked.

"Yes, it passes under fourteen bridges. And it divides the city into two big parts. These are the Left and Right Banks." Nicole pointed to two sides of the river. "The Left Bank has universities, artists, many cafés. The Right Bank has more government buildings and museums."

"And there's *Nôtre Dame* (Nohtrah Dahm) Cathedral on that island in the Seine," Miss Lake told the kids.

"Yes, that is called the *Île de la Cité* (eel duh lah sitay)," Nicole said. "This is where Paris first began – more than 2,100 years ago! A tribe of fishermen called the Parisii lived on this island because it could be protected from enemies."

"Now Paris has more than 9 million people! And it all began on the one little island," Miss

Lake said.

"Lisa, come over and see all of this," Amy called to her friend.

"If the swaying ever stops!" Lisa yelled. She stood up from her bench. Suddenly she looked down. "What's this! I was sitting on this envelope! And it's got our names on it!"

"A clue! Open it!" Justin told her.

Lisa tore open the envelope and read:

Are you hungry?

Come have lunch.

Float the river

While you munch!

"Hooray! We eat!" yelled Justin. "You see, Lisa, you *are* a good clue finder!"

21

CHAPTER 3

Lunch on the River

"Where can we float the river and still have lunch?" Amy asked Nicole.

"Sounds like the Bateau Mouche (bat-o moushe) to me!" their guide said. "That is a boat that docks near the bottom of this tower. Ready to go down?"

Lisa was first onto the elevator.

Soon they were down at the base. Then they followed Nicole over towards the river. Many big boats were docked along the bank.

They all had lots of seats, with glass roofs and sides. A man was waving an American flag in front of one boat.

"*Bonjour* (Bonsjure), Philippe (fill-eep)," Nicole called to him. "Are you ready for us?"

"*Oui* (we), I hope you are hungry! Welcome aboard, everyone!" Philippe said.

Everybody climbed onto the boat and sat at tables by the windows. A few other passengers were already seated.

"We are going up the river to the Louvre Museum," Nicole said. "It is not a long ride. But there is a lot to see. And you will have a delicious lunch as we go!"

"That sounds great to me!" said Justin.

"I've run out of *croissants*."

The boat started slowly up the river. Baskets of golden brown rolls appeared on the lunch tables. Then came *quiches* (keeshes). These were custard pies filled with ham and cheese.

"The first building you see to the right is the *Invalides,* (an-va-leeds)," Nicole said. "This is Napoléon's tomb. His body is buried in six small coffins there. Two silver containers hold his heart and stomach. To be buried this way was a great honor."

"Suddenly I'm not hungry!" Lisa said.

"Can we go see the tomb?" Justin asked.

"Yes. We'll make a list of all the places you

want to go," Nicole said. "Oh, look! There is one of the river barges that families live on. They are all waving to us!"

The kids waved to the family standing on the long flat boat. There was washing hung out to dry on a line. And barking dogs ran back and forth on the deck.

"These families live their whole lives on the river," said Miss Lake. "Look! We're going under our first bridge!"

"Do we have enough room? It's so low," Amy said. She looked ahead at the old stone bridge that curved gently over the river.

"We made it! No crunch!" Justin said.

"Look out on your left side now," Nicole

said. "You can see a little of the *Place* (plasse) *de la Concorde* where the guillotine was."

"Let's come back here for sure," said Juan. "Wow, that place sure looks big!"

"It is! And I want you to see the *Tuileries* (twee-ler-ees)," Nicole said. "Those are the gardens over there. They got their name because 500 years ago this was where workers dug up clay to make *tuiles,* or tiles."

Amy suddenly jumped up from the table. "I found a clue! It was under my water glass!"

CHAPTER 4

A Mysterious Lady

She is famous for her smile;

Once you find her, sit awhile.

"Leonardo" is the key

Say it to the guard and see!

"What smile? What a weird clue!" said Justin.

"And what guard?" asked Amy.

"Remember we talked about the famous paintings Paris has?" said Miss Lake.

"Do you mean the ones in the Louvre

Museum?" asked Lisa.

"Yes, and one has the famous smile!" said Juan. "So we just find her!"

"The Louvre has 8 miles of art!" said Miss Lake. "That might take awhile."

"What was her name? The lady in the painting?" Lisa asked.

"Funny *you* should ask that question, Lisa," laughed her teacher.

"Mona Lisa! That was her name! Now I remember," Lisa said.

"And Leonardo da Vinci painted her," Justin said. "Leonardo's a word in the clue."

"And the guard will give us our next clue!" Juan said.

The boat was slowly pulling over to the side of the river.

Everybody thanked Philippe and stepped onto the shore.

"I loved the boat ride," Amy said. "It helped me know where I am in Paris. On the métro you don't see where you're going."

"You are right. The Seine is the best way to see Paris," Nicole said. "Well, there's the Louvre ahead of you! Isn't it huge?"

"Totally gigantic!" Juan said.

They looked up at the great stone palace. It seemed to stretch for miles.

"Let's go find the Mona Lisa!" Juan said. "I want to see our next clue!"

"You are going to love your surprise in Paris." Nicole smiled mysteriously.

Finally they reached the Louvre courthouse and went up the curving staircase into the Louvre.

"We'll see the *Venus de Milo* first," Nicole said.

"Remember we studied the Venus, kids?" Miss Lake asked. "I bet you remember her."

"There she is!" Lisa said. She pointed to a tall white marble statue of a woman. Many people were grouped around it.

"Isn't she beautiful?" asked Nicole. "She was found on the Greek island of Milos in 1820. See how graceful her body is."

"What happened to her arms?" Lisa asked.

"No one knows," Nicole said. "Remember she is over 2000 years old!"

They all followed Nicole down the hall until they came to a room full of paintings.

Suddenly Lisa cried, "I see her!" She walked slowly towards the painting. "I can't believe it — this is the real Mona Lisa!"

"And there's the guard," Justin said.

"We have to sit for awhile first," Amy said. "Remember what the clue said?"

They all sat down on some benches in front of the Mona Lisa.

Leonardo da Vinci painted her in the early 1500's," Nicole said.

"Who was she?" Lisa asked.

"She was the wife of a nobleman from Florence, Italy," Nicole said. "What do you think of this painting?"

"It's hard to tell what she's thinking," Justin said. "Is she happy or sad?"

"That's what everyone wants to know," Nicole answered. "Her smile is mysterious."

"Look, that man is painting a picture of her. Isn't that against the law?" Juan pointed to a man who had brought his own set of paints to the museum.

"No," Nicole said. "It is allowed. Artists come here all the time to copy paintings. And some are very good!"

"Have we sat long enough?" Juan asked.

"I think so," Nicole said. "Are you ready to tell the guard the key word, Juan?"

"Yes!" Juan went over to the guard by the Mona Lisa. "Leonardo!" he said loudly and clearly.

The guard smiled. "You are getting near to your surprise!" he told the kids. Then he gave Juan a little envelope.

Juan ripped it open quickly. Then he read:

Gar-gar, they whisper in the rain;

On twin towers, near the Seine,

One of these monsters has the clue

To a big surprise for all of you!

CHAPTER 5

The Secrets of Notre Dame

"Gar-gar! What does that mean? And who are these monsters?" Juan asked.

"Where are twin towers by the Seine?" asked Amy.

"It's our hardest clue yet!" said Lisa.

Justin took his guidebook out of his backpack. "I'm going to look for something with twin towers," he said. The rest of the kids looked over his shoulder. They flipped through the pages of pictures.

Suddenly Justin said, "There! I bet that's it. Nôtre Dame Cathedral. See the twin towers? And it's right by the Seine river."

"Shall we go check it out?" asked Nicole. She smiled mysteriously. "We can take the métro to Nôtre Dame. Follow me!"

They all started for the métro. The ride seemed very fast.

"Here's our stop – Île de la Cité," said Miss Lake. "We're almost to Nôtre Dame."

"Remember that Paris began on this tiny island," Nicole told the kids. "But the cathedral wasn't completed until 1345. It took nearly 200 years to build!"

They all got off the métro and walked

upstairs to the street. The twin towers of Notre Dame rose up high in front of them.

"It's beautiful!" Amy said. "So huge!"

"See how it has three main big doors in front," Nicole said. "And look at the stained glass rose window in the center. It is more than 30 feet wide and 700 years old!"

"Many kings and queens were crowned here," Miss Lake said. "And the Emperor Napoléon! The church holds 6,500 people!"

"How high are those towers?" Juan asked. "That's where the monsters are with our clue!"

"The towers are 226 feet high," Nicole said. "One has a 13-ton bell."

"Have you kids ever heard of Victor Hugo's

book *The Hunchback of Nôtre Dame*? It was written back in 1840."

"Sounds pretty scary," said Lisa.

"The hero of the book was called Quasimodo," their teacher said. "He was a King Kong-type character and it was his job to ring the big bell."

"This is just make-believe, right?" Lisa asked.

"No, Lisa. The hunchback is still up there with the monsters," Justin laughed. "Better stay out of the tower!"

CHAPTER 6

The Monsters' Clue

"Let's go up now to see the bell," Nicole said. "I think it's about to rain!"

"Great! Let's find our clue!" Juan said.

"But what if the monsters don't want to give it to us?" Justin laughed.

"Follow me!" Nicole led them towards a side door of the cathedral.

"I think our clue will be hard to find," Amy said. "I sure don't get it – monsters that make a gar-gar sound."

"Mrs. X sure makes us work for our surprises!" Justin said. "Long stairs!"

"It's your backpack full of food!" Lisa called back to him down the stairs.

"No, it's empty now!" Justin laughed.

In a moment they stepped out onto an open platform. A gentle rain was falling.

"Wow! We're high!" Juan said. He stood at the railing looking down.

"Look at these weird stone things on the corners. Are they supposed to be animals? They're kind of scary-looking," Amy said.

"They are called gargoyles," Nicole said. "Some are demons. Others are animals and birds. I always think they are laughing as they look down at people!"

"Come and see the huge bell," Miss Lake said. "It weighs 13 tons!"

"O.K. Where are these monsters up here?" Juan wanted to know.

"The clue said they whisper in the rain. We should hear them now," Justin said.

"Maybe we need to be quiet a minute," Miss Lake said. "So we can listen."

"I just hear rain," Juan said after a minute. "I think we're in the wrong place."

"Wait! I hear a sort of gurgling sound," Lisa said. "It's coming from the gargoyles! Rain is coming out of their mouths."

"Yes, I hear it! Could this be the gar-gar

sound they whisper?" asked Amy.

"That's it! The gargoyles are the monsters!" Justin cried. "Fantastic!"

"But we haven't found the clue yet," Juan said. "Which one of these monsters has it?"

"Let's check them all," said Justin. "I'll start with this awful-looking monkey."

"I can deal with monsters like this," Lisa laughed. She made a face at one of the creatures who was sticking out its tongue.

"Nicole, please give us a clue!" Amy said. "We've got a lot of gargoyles to check."

Nicole just laughed. "I am having so much fun watching you search!"

"I'm about to give up!" Justin said.

"That's it! The gargoyles are the monsters,"
Justin cried.

"Wait! I think there's something here!" Amy had her hand under the back wings of a huge stone bird. "Yes! The clue! It was taped up under these wings!"

Amy slowly opened the little envelope. She began to read:

You've worked hard to win your prize

Now a treat awaits your eyes,

Tunnels dark with skulls so white,

You'll tour them with Nicole tonight!

"Skulls! Dark tunnels! Yikes! Where are you taking us, Nicole?" Lisa asked.

"Have you ever heard of the Catacombes of Paris?" Nicole asked the kids. "The Catacombes are underground burial places. The skeletons

43

were brought there from other cemeteries. It's really fun to take flashlights and explore all the different rooms. Easy to get lost!"

Now *this* is a neat surprise!" said Juan. "Thank you, Mrs. X!"

"I think I want *two* flashlights on this trip!" Lisa said. "Just to make sure!"

"Are there postcards of the Catacombes? I want to send one to Mrs. X!" Justin said.

"I don't know," laughed Nicole. "But if they do I am sure we can find one. Now, let's get out of this rain! Who's ready for a snack before we see the cathedral?" asked Nicole.

"Did you say snack?" asked Justin. "Where are those stairs? I'm outta here!"